This book was written for the fun of reading........enjoy!

Keep an eye out for the mouse on every page!

Chapters

Chapter 1

Arguing wi' Mum

Smiley and his Mum, Wolley, were having a
serious chat about him moving out.

"I only have 200 Bigley Wogleys, will you lend
me another 50? Pwwwwease?" pleaded Smiley.
"What do you think I am, made of money?"
yelled Wolley.
"No, I thought you were a witch!" Smiley
answered cheekily but truthfully.

"Quiet toothless boy or I'll turn you into a mouse!" yelled Wolley, this time with steaming ears. She always called Smiley toothless because he was the only vampire ever to be born with no fangs.
Smiley thought for a moment and decided to put on the petted lip to try and get the extra money from his mum. It usually worked.

"B-B-B-But Mum, I-I-I won't be able to get a house with o-o-only 200 Bigley Wogleys!" he whimpered.
"Ok, ok I'll give you 10, that'll have to do" she never could resist the petted lip.
"30?" Smiley asked hopefully.
"20 and that's my final offer boy!" declared Wolley."Ok, 20 would be great, thanks Mum" Smiley sighed, not wanting to sound ungrateful.

Chapter 2
The Gnomes

Meanwhile across town, two Gnomes were
writing a letter for their Mum.

They live in the centre of NogNog.
Their names were Rupert and Roger.
They live in two small caves. One was
big, bumpy and dirty, that was the home of
Rupert.

The other was small, smooth and very,
very clean and tidy, (so tidy you would think it
was a show cave!) that was the home of Roger.
They were very excited because there was a
dance soon and everyone in NogNog was invited,
even them!
Roger had decided they had better write down
when and where it was so that Dear Mother
could go too, (she was quite forgetful!).
"We'll write down the information for Dear
Mother, and will go and visit her later today to
give it to her." said Roger, as he was the one
with all the clever ideas. He handed Rupert a
pencil and a grubby piece of paper and Rupert
started to write as Roger dictated.......

Chapter 3
Princess Messymooth and Toad

Princess Messymooth (who was called
Princess by her dad, the Mayor of NogNog,
and thought everyone else should call her that too)
was fastening on her Tuesday bib, when she heard
a faint knock on the door.

"'Chomp, Chomp. Just a minute, Chomp." she
shouted mid-chew (she was always eating).
"Hello." croaked Toad, in his most dashing voice
when she finally answered the door.
"Hello." replied Princess, while forcing
another twenty humbugs into her mouth.
"Why are you here?" she slobbered.
"Why? Because I need a kiss." Puckered Toad.

"And what will happen if I do kiss you?" asked
the princess curiously whilst devouring a toffee.
"I will turn into your wildest most fantastic
dream!" answered Toad very energetically.

"Ooh la la, a raspberry ripple cake with cream!
mmmmmmmmmmmm!" yelled the princess in
delight (and half in-dream).
"NO!" screeched Toad in dismay, "I'll turn into a
handsome Prince!"

Chapter 4
The Slobbery Sticky Kiss of Sadness

"Ok" agreed the princess, "As long as you're
handsome."
"I will be." replied the excited Toad.
So Princess closed her eyes and
puckered up, as did Toad.
Their lips met, and Princess opened her eyes to
see the prince that should
be standing before her.....

"NOTHING HAPPENED!" She screamed "YOU HORRIBLE SLIMY TOAD YOU... GO AWAY!!!!!" And with that she slammed the door in the most furious fashion.

Toad turned away and murmured "I will be back and next time you will be my Princess, no one will stop me from being ruler of NogNog – NO ONE!"

Chapter 5

In Love

Smiley jumped into his coffin car. He
was going to find a house with his now 220
Bigley Wogleys.
He had only driven a short while when all of a
sudden he jammed on his brakes.

"Oh what pretty flower do I see before me?"
He vaulted out of his car and ran up to Princess
Messymooth (who had decided to go for a walk
to calm herself down after the trouble with Toad.)

"Who are you?" exclaimed Princess in surprise,
a dribble of spit trickling down her chin due to
the overflow of sweets stuffed into her mouth.
"I am Smiley Googleudder Toestopper, and you
are?...""I am Princess Messymooth, but you may
call me Princess!" she smiled.
Smiley was in love!

Chapter 6
Invitation

Princess Messymooth thought Smiley was a nice vampire, if a little strange!

"Would you like to come to the NogNog village dance with me on Saturday?" she asked.
"I-I-I would love to" Smiley stuttered in shock.

"Good, I look forward to it" said Princess happily "You may pick me up at seven from 6 NogNog place." And with that Princess continued her walk.

"So will I!" Smiley called after her, with his big fang-less smile. He stared after 'Messy' not believing that he had a date with such a beautiful girl. "Seven at 6 NogNog place it is." he said to himself. He hopped back into his coffin car with a great big grin.

Chapter 7

The House

After a lot of driving Smiley finally came across an old house. It was falling apart. It had a big hole in the chimney, bricks missing from the walls and a wonky door, but Smiley knew it was the only thing he could afford. Not only did he presume it would be cheap, it was also the closest place in NogNog to Princess Messymooth (apart from the old Gnomes' houses).

Smiley knocked on the door, scared to knock too hard in case his new home-to-be fell to pieces.

A little elf answered the door looking very tired and covered in sweat.

"Can I help you, I'm kind of busy just now as you can probably tell?" panted the elf.

"Oh, sorry..." said Smiley "but I happened to notice your house was for sale... and was wondering how much you were selling it for?" smiley pointed to the 'For Sale' sign in the garden.

"221 Bigley Wogleys." Said the elf rather bluntly.

"I only have 220..." pleaded Smiley.

"Well it looks like you'll have to get your skates on to get that 1 Bigley Wogley or you're going to be too late. There are other people wanting this house you know and if you don't hurry they just might snap it up before you." The elf stated cruelly, laughing at what he had just said. He slammed the door, right in Smiley's face. "I don't even have skates." said Smiley rather disheartened as he made his way back to his coffin car.

Chapter 8

A Mouse in the House

Back in the old crumbling house, the elf
continued to sweat, trying to catch a mouse (he
thought he'd better since he was trying to sell
the house!) but actually catching the mouse was
a lot more difficult than he had originally
thought.
Not only because of the fact that the mouse was
almost as big as he was, but also because it was
a lot more clever than he had realised.

The elf had tried hitting the mouse with a broom (made of a matchstick) to scare it away. He'd tried cornering it to catch it, he'd tried setting a trap with cheese to tempt it. However, no matter what he tried, squashing, killing, catching and even tricking, the mouse always managed to outsmart him and get away. He spent all day trying to catch the mouse but nothing was working.

"Never mind, you won't be my problem much longer if that silly looking, fangless fellow comes back with the money." And with that the elf gave up.

Chapter 9
Dooms Day

Smiley stopped his car at a nice spot at the foot of Buleump's hill. He decided to walk up the hill a wee bit to give him a chance to think. He thought a moment about how he was going to get another one Bigley Wogley. He thought and thought about it but just couldn't think of a way that he could get the money. So Smiley, feeling hopeless, walked back down the hill toward his coffin car. Suddenly, disaster struck...

A sudden and out of the blue bolt of lightning
came out of the sky and struck Smiley's
little pee sized brain and he fell to the floor.
Dead!
(but don't worry too much,
NogNog has a really good doctor, of sorts...)

Chapter 10

The Shock

The two gnomes were walking to Dear Mother's house to give her the invitation for the party, when they came across a body lying limp on the road.

"Dead as a door knob!" They exclaimed.
"Quick call an ambulance, poor creature needs help!" yelled Roger.

Rupert sprang into action and ran across the road to the public phone box and started to dial the number for the ambulance service to take the creature to Doc McDead's infirmary... However, the next moment Roger looked across, and there was Rupert laying passed out in the phone box! The whole event had proven too stressful.

"Great" Roger exclaimed. "I have to do everything around here."

Chapter 11
The Phone Call

'Bring Bring...Bring Bring...'
"Hello this is the emergency service how may I help you?" sighed the operator sounding completely bored.

"Eeemmmmm... I'm not quite sure how to put this, but my brother and I were walking along the road near Buleump's hill."

"We found a creature lying there, dead,
as a door knob, then my brother
Rupert came to call you and he passed
out in the phone box...
Do you think youwould be able to
send the ambulance as quick
as possible to help us?" Roger pleaded.
"I'll get onto it right away." The operator stated,
still in a somewhat bored fashion.

Chapter 12
The Ambulance

The ambulance came speeding along the road (doing 4 miles per hour) with the sirens screaming. Eventually they reached the dead-as-a-dodo Smiley.

Two wizards hopped out of the banged-up ambulance. A tall and rather skinny wizard turned to Rupert, who had now come round and managed to pick himself up, and asked "So what may the problem be here?" "Well" said Rupert, "We were simply walking along the road to Dear Mother's house to give her information about the party on Saturday..." "What party is that?" The wee plump wizard (named Tubby by all who knew him) rudely interrupted.

"You know the party that the whole of NogNog are invited to... Even me and Roger!!!" replied Rupert.

"Really?" said Tubby "I have heard nothing of this party!"

"Oh you need to come... it's going to be the BEST party EVER" Rupert said in delight.

"Excuse me!" said the tall wizard looking quite stern (as usual) he went by the name of Lanky Joe. "Could we please get back to the matter at hand of what happened to this poor creature?!"

"Oh yes, sorry" Rupert continued "well we were walking along to Dear Mother's house, when out of nowhere this creature appeared in the road... like magic, it appeared!"

"No no no no ... that's not what happened at all." Roger stated "We were walking along and there was a massive bang and a puff of smoke and there lay that creature. Amazing, some weird things happen in this town I tell you... just wait until I tell everyone."

"That's not what happened at all." exclaimed Lanky Joe. "This 'creature', As you all put it, is a young vampire without fangs, and he happens to be called Smiley Googleudder Toestopper... Very nice young man he was, knew his dad. It seems, after a very basic examination that Smiley has been struck by lightning and has died. Real shame... Good boy was Smiley... always smiling. Doc McDead will be able to help though, I'm sure of it. Works wonders that Imp.

Chapter 13
The Journey

"Ok Tubby get the stretcher out." Ordered
Lanky Joe.
"Right away Lanky Joe." Answered Tubby
So the wizards strapped Smiley into the
stretcher and put him in the back of the
ambulance.

"Off we go then. Doc McDead will be most interested in seeing the new arrival." Said Lanky Joe. With that, the Ambulance doors were slammed shut and the ambulance flew off at 3 miles per hour... sirens screaming!

"BIG GREY HARD THINGS COMING UP!" yelled Tubby.

"THERE ROCKS YOU HALFWIT!" Shouted Lanky Joe with anger in his voice and blood shot eyes. "Now let's get on with the journey and BE QUIET!"

"Ok J..." Tubby started to say but was cut off by Joe... "SHHSHHSHHSHHSHHSHHSHHSHH!"

Thud, Thud, Thud, Thud, went the ambulance as it sped over the rocks.

"Next stop, Doc McDeads infirmary!" said Joe, this time a bit more happily.

Chapter 14
Doc McDead

The ambulance slammed its brakes on and came to a complete halt. Tubby ended up on the dashboard, with his bottom in the air. The two wizards unloaded Smiley from the back of the ambulance. Before they got him out Tubby thought he would try and wake him up by smashing his head off the door (it didn't work). Joe sneezed, and a great big blob of green snot went hurtling towards Tubby and went right down the back of his throat (as he was yawning). Tubby started to choke and slobber (which he was good at) and he coughed up the biggest ball of gunk you have ever seen. It flew through the air and splattered against the ambulance window.

As he had been eating garlic
and eggs for breakfast that morning, the smell
also flew through the air, killing the flies that
were buzzing about the dead body of Smiley,
and it also made Joe's face turn a peculiar
shade of green.

"Let's get this corpse inside and quick, it STINKS!"
said Tubby.

They smashed through the door of the hospital, ran over two nurses, one sick patient and a wheelchair but eventually made it to Doc McDeads infirmary.

"Doctor!Doctor! Smileys dead!" yelled the two wizards in unison, a little out of breath.

"Smiley who?" asked the doctor (he was a very small imp who had half a teapot for a head, but we don't discuss that, it's a very touchy subject!)

""Smiley, from the old caravan. You know, that goofy vampire with no fangs and hair with so much gel it's like slime? He really should cut down on the gel." said Tubby "but I guess that doesn't matter now."

"Shut up!" said Joe in an angry whisper.

"Oh of course, that guy!" Doc McDead said while finishing off his cup of very strong coffee.

Tubby and Joe flopped Smiley onto the
surgery bed with a great 'CRASH'.
Doc McDead came over to Smiley
with an electric drill and a huge circular saw.

"Time for your surgery boy." Doc McDead said
with a little giggle at the end. McDead grabbed
the circular saw and pulled the cord, the engine
roared, 'DROOM, DROOM, DROOM!'
"Seems to me this old chap is dead! But not to
worry, we can use the old formula and a bit of
elbow grease and he'll be wrong as rain!"
Doc McDead x-rayed the body of Smiley, he
saw a spanner, an elastic band and an old boot
with a knotted lace and a buckled sole.
He carried on with the operation, he used jump
leads (from the ambulance) to start his heart
again (after putting down the saw of course.)

35

Soon after, seven or eight attempts with the
jump leads, the monitors started to bleep (I
won't explain how he got to the heart, it's a bit
gruesome, but it did involve the saw!) but
Smileys eyes did not open.

So Doc McDead picked up the electric drill and
powered it up. He cracked open Smileys skull
like a nut and found a big button that read...
'Push me, I'll blink'

Doc McDead paused for a moment and thought to himself, "I wonder what this button does?" He pushed it and Smileys eyes shot open like a till. He looked over Smiley, his eyes were open, his heart was beating but he still wasn't moving. "What could have gone wrong?" McDead muttered to himself puzzled.

"EUUUREKAA!" he yelled so loudly that all his staff got a shock (they almost jumped out of their skin!). "The lungs! I know just what to do." He jumped into the already open body of Smiley and started pounding his lungs until they started working again. McDead quickly clambered out and sewed the body back together with his super-duper sewing machine.

"There we are." Doc McDead said happily, dusting off his hands.

Smiley woke up slowly "OUCH!" he squealed.
Eventually Smiley thanked Doc McDead and
headed out of the hospital, (feeling a little
wobbly on his feet). He was away to visit his
Mum again to explain about the house and see
if she could help (again).

Chapter 15
Dad's Comin' Home

At exactly the same time that Smiley was leaving the hospital a plane was flying over NogNog, and it looked like it was going to be coming in for a landing at Wolley's caravan (remember, she was Smiley's Mum!). But what no one knew was that on the plane was a very special but unexpected visitor. Mr Mammoth Googleudder Toestopper!

Chapter 16
The Crash Landing

The plane that Mr Mammoth Googleudder
Toestopper was on went hurtling towards
Wolley's caravan at 260mph (tee hee, only
joking) at 12 miles an hour, and crashed into
the tree right outside. Wolley ran outside "MY
TREE, MY BEAUTIFUL BAT TREE!" she sobbed,
but then her sadness almost immediately
turned into anger. She started to stride over to
the pilot to give him a piece of her mind. She
looked very scary when she was angry (the green
face mask didn't help!) but before she reached
the plane Mr Mammoth stepped out and said
"Honey, sugar-plum!". Wolley turned around,
showing her green facemask that she used to
keep her skin nice and horrible and he
screamed with fright

"A-A-A-A-A-A-R-R-G-G-H-H-H-H-H,
WE'RE BEING ATTACKED BY ALIENS
FROM PLANET ZOGGINS!"
"No, No, you silly old fool, it's me Wolley. Is it
really you Mammoth?" she asked, not really
believing her eyes, she could still remember him
leaving to go banjo playing and to see more than
NogNog many years ago.

"Yes my little bat dropping, it is me!"

They hugged, ecstatic to see each other
again after all these years.
Wolley's face was beginning to look
like it was melting as her face mask was
beginning to slide off, and big green globules
were dripping down Mammoths back, but they
were happy and together again at last.

Chapter 17

Lookin' Back

Smiley
age 1

Wolley and Mammoth went into the caravan
to have a chat with a cup of coffee and some
mouldy biscuits. Wolley told him all about
Smiley getting a house (or trying to!) and feeling
guilty, Mammoth offered to help Smiley move
his things to his new house when he got it, he
felt it was the least he could do.

Wolley remembered 'Ye old photo album' and decided it was a good time to have a look back at some old memories. It was really nice apart from that piece of gum at the top right-hand corner, and all those blasted spelling errors.
"What happened to the boy's face in that pic?" asked Mammoth concerned, Smiley looked like a tomato in it, and his face was all swollen and red.
"We bought a cat to get rid of some rats, but it turned out he was severely allergic." replied Wolley, never once taking her eyes off of Mammoth.
"I'm so glad you came back!" said Wolley fluttering her eyelashes and looking at him with big Goo Goo eyes.

Mammoth had a tear in his eye,
he couldn't believe how much of his son's
life he had missed, but he was
here to stay this time!

Chapter 18
Dear Mother

Roger and Rupert walked to Dear Mother's house (after all the excitement with Smiley, they still had a message to deliver) but as soon as they got there the door swung open and Dear Mother wobbled out yelling "ROGER, RUPERT, WHAT A SURPRISE, COME IN! I'll fix you something to eat, you look starved." (They didn't look like they needed food at all!) "COME IN!"

Mother was a very large gnome lady. She was very round but you could just make out a pair of hairy feet and knobbly knees. Roger and Rupert followed their mum inside slowly, it had been a while since they had last seen her and they never really enjoyed their visits. Mother was very loud and Grandmother was, well, Grandmother.

Chapter 19

Mother's House

Roger and Rupert walked into the smelly,
dusty hovel of a cave. In the corner sat a
crooked old Gnome...

"GRANDMOTHER!" Rupert yelled in surprise.

"Cuthbert?" the old gnome answered in a dusty
voice.

"No Grandmother! I'm Rupert." He said.

"Oh yes, Cuthbert, now I remember." Said
Grandmother.

"IT'S RUPERT!" he yelled in anger, feeling quite
frustrated.

"No need to yell Cuthbert!" sighed Grandmother.

"GGGRRRRRR." Grumbled Rupert, and he
stormed off, slamming the door behind him.

"I may be old, but I know that you just walked
into the closet!" sniggered the old gnome.

Rupert came out with a red face and Roger
started to laugh. Rupert just scowled
(his cheeks were very red).
Dear Mother came in holding the note they
had brought her and shrieked in delight.
She read from the note "Everyone is invited to
the NogNog party on Saturday night, make sure
to dress fancy!"
"EEEEKKKK, A PARTY! I DO LOVE TO DRESS
UP, I CANT WAIT TO GO!"

Chapter 20
Mum's the Word

Smiley was on his way back from Doc McDead's to his mums. As he got closer to the caravan he saw his mum and someone he recognised standing outside (after he had noticed the huge plane that was smashed outside).

"DAD!" he shouted while running towards him, arms wide open, ready to give him a hug. Smiley was inches away from him when .... 'WALLOP' smiley smacked into and fell over the wall running around Wolleys caravan.

Wolley and Mammoth giggled, and Smiley got up with an embarrassed face.

Inside they all sat on the couch with
hot cups of coffee.
"Mum," Smiley said in a suspiciously
sweet tone,"you are looking uglier than ever!"
"What ya' wanting boy?" Wolley spat
questioningly.
"Emmm, another one Bigley Wogley?" whispered
Smiley hopefully.
"WHAT?!" she yelled
"Eh, anoth...." He didn't get to finish his
sentence as his Dad interrupted.

"You have to earn your Bigley Wogleys son. I will gladly help you move your things, but you have to figure out how to pay your own way in this world. Now get that drink down you and go earn it." Mammoth smiled.

Smiley drank his coffee and slumped off sadly, wondering what on earth he was going to do.

Chapter 21
Banjo Bonanza

Smiley walked and walked and thought and thought (you could almost hear the cogs turning in his brain). Suddenly he had a great idea, he would play the banjo, just like his dad.

"If my dad can make Bigley Wogleys playing the banjo, I'm sure I could do it too, but where am I going to get a banjo? ...THE DUMP!" so he sped of to try his luck, in search for a money-making banjo.

At the dump, he searched through many a pile of interesting rubbish, when eventually he came across a beautiful mouldy, fantastically crusty old banjo.

"YEEEESSSS!" he screamed in delight "It's beautiful, it's amazing, it's ... broken!" his face dropped, he had picked up the banjo and it had split into two pieces. "What am I going to do?" Smiley shook the banjo in frustration and as he did he heard a noise, 'THUMP, THUMP, THUMP' (a soft thudding noise was coming from inside) "I think there's something inside..." he looked "A sandwich, yummy."

CRUNCH, MUNCH...

While munching on the mouldy old cheese sandwich, Smiley got a sharp pain in his bottom teeth.

"OOUUUCCCCHHHHH!" he yelled in pain,
spitting out the mouthful of gloop on to the
ground. It wasn't until Smiley's eyes had
stopped watering with pain, that he noticed
something glinting up at him from the muck. It
was one shiny, slightly chewed Bigley Wogley!
He could now afford the house and live near
Princes Messymooth!

Chapter 22

The House 2

Smiley set off from the dump (not wanting to wait another second) in his coffin car at a tremendous speed of five miles per hour, towards the house that was soon to be his.

Once there, just as he switched off the engine, he saw her, like a giant chocolate covered angel, Princess Messymooth (she was obviously on her way home from the sweet shop!).

"H-H-H-Hi." He stammered.

"Hello again." She smiled with brown teeth (she had clearly just had a mouthful of chocolate.)

"Are we still on for the dance?" she inquired sweetly.

"Sure, I mean, of course!" he replied. Princess Messymooth gave him a girly, giggly sort of smile, and then continued on her way. Smiley knocked on the door and was invited in by the small elf. Once inside, Smiley noticed that the house was really dusty and kind of smelly, but Smiley still wanted it (we all know why!)

"Emm, I have something to tell you before you buy this house!" said the elf shiftily, "I am sorry Sir but in this house there is .... A mouse! Hee hee hee." He sniggered.

"What are you laughing at?" enquired Smiley.

"House, Mouse?.... I'm a poet and I didn't even know it, ha ha ha, I crack myself up." Giggled the elf.

"I don't care, nothing will stop me buying this house!" stated Smiley, "I'll buy it."
"SOLD!" Yelled the elf jumping from one foot to the other.

Chapter 23
Moving Co.

After making the deal with the elf (and getting the keys) Smiley was back in his coffin car and heading back to his Mum's for the last time, to get his things.

Smiley ran into the caravan in such a rush, as he was so excited, that he squashed his Dad behind the door when he threw it open. "I GOT THE HOUSE, I GOT THE HOUSE!" he yelled.

"Well done boy" said his father while straightening out his squashed nose, "You had better phone the moving company and I'll help you move your things out."

Smiley picked up the phone and dialled the number for 'Moving Co.

'BRING-BRING BRING-BRING'-"Hello, this is Moving Co. ready to help you move" said the operator.

Smiley thought that the operator sounded like they had a bit of a cold, or they were very, very bored!

"Emmm, Hello, this is Smiley Googleudder Toestopper, I would like you to come to NogNog village, number 2, Wolley's caravan today please. My Dad and I are going to need your help moving my things to my new home."

"No problem mister 'googly-toe' we'll be right with you." Smiley hung up then rushed off to pack.

Chapter 24

The Goblin

Smiley was walking back and forth in the
caravan (there was almost a hole
worn into the carpet!)
suddenly the doorbell rang...
'DING-DONG, DING-DONG' Smiley rushed to
the door.
"Hello, I'm Smiley, do come in." he said very
politely, if a bit quick.
Smiley was very surprised as the goblin was not
at all what he thought he would be like. He was
fat, bald, and had a patch on his left eye, there
was also six stitches on his stomach and a
tattoo on his right arm which read 'MOMMY'.

Chapter 25
Pack Up

Smiley showed the goblin into his bedroom where his Dad had just finished packing his things into boxes.

The goblin saw all of Smiley's things before him, amongst the boxes were...

A big king-sized bed, sixteen pots of half-used hair gel (most of which had been bought that morning – Smiley used it like it was going out of fashion!), a broken mirror, some trousers and capes, a table and an old rocking chair.

Smiley slapped on some more gel while the goblin and his Dad packed his things into the removal van (it didn't take too long).

Smiley said good bye to his Mum and Dad
(his Mum cried, that didn't happen often!) and
set off to his new home, to start his new
independent life.

Chapter 26
A New Home

Smiley arrived at his new home
(we'll use the term 'new' very loosely!)
"Just put my things in that room over there
please." Said Smiley excitedly.
'CRASH'
"All done" said the goblin in a very bored tone,
and he left.

Smiley started sorting out his boxes of
belongings when he heard a noise which
sounded like it was coming from the wall. He
crept over to listen closer, his ear pressed
against the wall.
'SCRAPE, SCRAPE'
It was then he remembered the elf telling him
about a mouse.

Just as he moved away from the wall, a mouse
scurried out from the hole.
"EEEEEEKKKKKKKK!" Smiley squealed while
hopping about.
The mouse just stopped and looked at him, then
it started laughing (well it was squeaking, as
mice do, but it certainly looked like it was
laughing.)

"You're not scared are you?" asked Smiley, feeling a bit silly as he was speaking to a mouse, but then the mouse shook its head.

"You can understand me?" questioned Smiley in shock.

The mouse nodded and then rubbed its tummy in a very sad manor.

"You're hungry? I'll see what I have for you, hold on!"

Smiley returned with a bit of cheese and a crumb of cracker, the mouse scoffed the lot greedily. "Maybe it won't be too bad to have you around little mouse, we'll both have some company." Smiley grinned a fangless grin, and the mouse followed him as Smiley continued sorting out his new home.

Chapter 27
Toad's Plan

Meanwhile at Toads bog, Toad was pacing back and forward on a lily pad, still fuming from the Princess Messymooth, kiss incident.

"I know I'm supposed to be a Prince, not a toad. I just don't understand what happened?! If I kiss a Princess I should be transformed into a handsome Prince and I will rule all of Nognog, why didn't it work???"

He had thought and thought and pondered and pondered ever since the kiss and just couldn't figure out what had gone wrong.

"I KNOW! She has to be attracted to me before the kiss, that's it! Who's going to want to kiss a toad, 'CROAK'. She wanted a raspberry ripple cake, I'll give her a raspberry ripple cake and a Prince all in one!

I will rule NogNog, I WILL HA
HA HA HA HA!"
Toad was so excited he fell off the pad and into
the water. SPLASH!

He slowly appeared out of the water covered in
weeds and feeling a bit sheepish, all the insects
and creatures nearby that had seen it happen
started to roll about laughing and pointing.
"SHUT UP!" bellowed Toad, then muttered
under his breath "Just you wait until that
stupid party when my plan will be unveiled,
then we'll see who's laughing!"

With that he stormed inside his sad little home
(it was made of lily pads and weeds)
and slammed the door.
He had to prepare the details of his evil master
plan for taking over NogNog.

Chapter 28
New Friends

It had been three days since Smiley had moved into his house, he had become great friends with squeak (that's what he decided to name the mouse, it was a cute name for a cute, small white mouse and it squeaked a lot!) He had finished unpacking and had even bumped into Princess Messymooth.

"I can't believe the party is tomorrow Squeak, I'm so nervous, what should I wear? How should I do my hair? Should I get her a gift?!" Smiley asked, so quickly that he didn't even take a breath and was starting to turn blue with lack of air by the end.

Squeak just looked up at Smiley with interest.

"You'll come with me won't you?... for support?"
Smiley asked pleadingly.
Squeak nodded.

Chapter 29
Princess

It was the night of the party, Smiley and Squeak
were just about ready to leave to pick up Princess.
Smiley just checked to make sure
he had done everything.
He had his coffin car keys, had told
his Mum and Dad about the party and
had even cleaned the coffin car.
He had decided to wear his red and white suit
that had the red, silk cape and had used
even more gel than usual. 74

"I think we're ready, let's go." He said quite nervously.

Smiley and Squeak pulled up at Princess Messymooth's house (after two seconds of driving).

"Well I better go get her." Smiley gulped so hard that it sounded like he was trying to swallow an apple whole.

'BING BONG, BING BONG' Went the door-bell. It felt like ages that Smiley was standing waiting, when the door finally opened.

"You- you look beautiful!" stammered Smiley. The princess was wearing a floor length dress that was a beautiful baby blue colour, and she had a lollipop in her hair holding it all up.

"Thank you." She said sweetly, and she was blushing slightly.

Squeak was sitting on Smileys shoulder.
Princess simply smiled and petted the mouse on
the head, then started walking toward the coffin
car.
"Shall we go?" she asked once sitting in the car.
"Lets." Smiley said with a huge smile on his
face.

Chapter 30
The Party

Smiley and Princess arrived at the town hall and walked in, hand in hand (apart from when he was opening the door for Princess.) They picked a table near the dance floor as Princess liked to dance. Smiley fetched a couple of drinks (including a thimble full for Squeak) of Lanky Joe's famous fruit punch.

"Shall we dance?" asked Princess.

"Ok." Said Smiley and they took to the dance floor. Once Smiley got more comfortable and relaxed, he really started to enjoy himself. The music was great, the buffet was full of all his favourite foods: purple carrot sticks with dip, red jacket potatoes filled with things like frogs eggs, out of date cheese and other such yummy things, and there was even a raspberry ripple cake, Messy's favourite!

It must have kept getting moved though
as every time he looked over it was
in a different place.
The thing Smiley was enjoying the most though,
was his time with Princess Messymooth. They
eventually took a seat again and had a drink of
the punch as they were both quite tired from all
the energetic dancing they had been doing. Just
as they sat down the door sprung open and a
rather large gnome lady dressed as a large,
green bush followed by the two gnomes burst
into the hall. It was Rupert and Rodger with
their Dear Mother. They were dressed as
flowers, one was yellow and the other was pink.
The music screeched to a halt and every person
in the hall looked over open mouthed at the
sight in front of them dressed
up like garden plants.

"I told you it wasn't a fancy dress party!"
squealed Roger in embarrassment.
Dear Mother spoke up "Oops, when the note
said to dress fancy I thought it meant fancy
dress!"
They just stood at the door for what seemed like
an eternity. Finally after a long, surprised pause
the music started again and everyone got back
to their drinks, (trying to stifle their giggles) as
the gnomes walked across the room slightly red
in the face.

Shortly after that embarrassing incident
Smiley's parents arrived, his Mum was wearing
a black and red dress which looked like spiders
webs, (it was her best dress) and his Dad was
wearing what he said was called a kilt. His parents
sat beside Smiley, Princess Messymooth and
Squeak.
"Well who is this charming young woman?
Smiley you never told me you had a lady friend."
asked Wolley nosily, but in a very polite voice (it
must have been because they were in the
company of Princess, Smiley thought).
"Emmmm, this is Princess Messymooth." Said
Smiley feeling quite embarrassed.

"PRINCESS!?" squealed Smiley's Dad.

Leaping forward to kiss her hand, in his haste
he nearly spilled all the drinks on the table
(apart from Squeaks, the mouse was
protecting it as though it was the last
fruit punch on earth)
"It's a pleasure to meet you my lady"
said Mammoth. Squeak soon got bored
of listening to the idle chit chat that was going
on at the table since Smiley's parents
had met Princess, and decided
to head over to the buffet table to grab some
food before it opened.
"BUFFET IS NOW OPEN!" the DJ yelled over the
music.
Princess Messymooth hauled her dress up and
was off like a shot straight to the sweet section.
"A RASPBERRY RIPPLE CAKE!" she screamed in
excitement and picked it up, the cream looked
delicious and dribbled down her chubby little
fingers.

She went to take a bite but it wasn't
until it was almost at her lips that she noticed a
pair of eyes staring back at her!

"EEEEEEEEEEEEAAAAAAKKKKKKKKK!" she
screamed, throwing the cake back on the table.
The whole room went silent. The cake stood up,
it was then that Princess realized something was
inside the cake!

"YOU! You slimy little toad, what are you
doing?!" she asked angrily.
"I am here for a kiss. I will be Prince of NogNog,
and as you can see I have gone to great lengths
to make myself more attractive for you."
Said Toad.
"I would never kiss you again you lying toad!"
she exclaimed. "Besides, I have a boyfriend now".
Smiley's cheeks turned red when she looked at
him and said this, he was her boyfriend.

"HIM?" yelled Toad. "He will not spoil my plan, I WILL be Prince!" Toad took one giant leap toward Smiley and pushed him over, he pulled something from the raspberry ripple cake he was hiding in.

"I have a big ball of cat hair here, and I know your precious 'boyfriend' is highly allergic to it, I have done my research. HAHAHAHA!" Toad chuckled evilly. Smiley's eyes widened in shock and fear. "You will kiss me or he will suffer the consequences." Toad demanded whilst wiggling the ball of cat hair nearer Smiley. Princess looked at Smiley and knew she had no choice. She walked slowly over to him and closed her eyes. Their lips almost touched when all of a sudden Squeak appeared out of nowhere and intercepted the kiss with mouse lips.

Everybody involved fell to the floor in shock, not
quite sure what had happened. Toad was the
most confused to find a mouse sitting on top of
him.
"WHAT IS GOING ON?" Toad screamed, but
without warning he started to wiggle and jiggle,
it looked like he was going to be sick, then he
started growing fur!
"WHAT IS HAPPENING TO ME?" Toad asked,
feeling scared and confused.

"It looks like he is turning in to a mouse!"
Squealed Wolley.

Toad had infact turned into a mouse, his green
skin had disappeared and he was now covered
in fluffy white fur.
"A mouse?" questioned Smiley feeling slightly
puzzled. "But that would have to mean that
Squeak was a girl! And a Princess at that!"
Squeak just nodded at Smiley, She was no other
than the Mouse Princess of NogNog.

"I think she likes him." Giggled Princess
Messymooth as Squeak looked lovingly at the
new Toad, in mouse form.

"NO, NO, NO. THIS WAS NOT PART OF THE
PLAN!" wailed Toad.

Squeak just looked at Toad and hugged him, Toad looked back at her pretty mouse eyes. "No one has ever hugged me before! You are quite beautiful, for a mouse. Maybe this mouse life won't be so bad after all. At least I'm a Prince. I knew it, I knew it." Toad said feeling much better by the end of his sentence.
Smiley was still shocked, he had had no idea that Squeak was a girl, never mind being the Princess of all the mice of NogNog.

Princess Messymouth took Smiley's hand lovingly "Shall we go and eat the buffet now?" She asked eyeing up the food-covered table. "Of course my love." He replied with a smile.

Chapter 31
Excitement Over

Princess Messymooth had decided to chat with Smiley after the party at his new home. They were cosy beside the fire, eating marshmallows, (Toad and Squeak were toasting marshmallows too). They were all talking about their future together and making things right. Smiley was the happiest he had ever been.

"I think I'm going to like it here." Smiled Toad. (His plan had worked out after all. He was the Prince of NogNog, granted a mouse prince, but a prince none the less and he had fallen in love with Squeak).
"I think I'll like it too, you being here." Squeaked Squeak. (Toad could understand her now he had changed into a mouse.) They all tucked into their toasted marshmallows.

Back at Wolley's caravan Mammoth and
Wolley were cuddled up on the couch. Mammoth
had decided to stay with Wolley in NogNog
forever, no more banjo playing.

The gnomes were all at Dear Mother's
house, still a little embarrassed about their
mistake with their choice of clothing earlier.

"Don't worry Cuthbert, everyone makes mistakes" said Grandmother.

"IT'S RUPERT!" He shouted.

"Ok Cuthbert, no need to shout, grumpy pants." Grandmother said, while heading slowly to bed.

And they all lived happily ever after!

Printed in Great Britain
by Amazon

84365014R00054